INTO THE
SCARY

William Anderson

authorHOUSE®

AuthorHouse™
1663 Liberty Drive
Bloomington, IN 47403
www.authorhouse.com
Phone: 833-262-8899

Published by AuthorHouse 09/01/2020

ISBN: 978-1-5462-6404-0 (sc)
ISBN: 978-1-5462-6403-3 (e)

Print information available on the last page.

To be scared is part of the human psyche which, I do say To be scared is a mental or pshycal reaction to some opposite force, real or imaginary. If you did a study on confucius youd find some knowledge on all types of things we do so master in this world. Confucius "what is there to.. fear?" id say alot sire and nothing at the same time. Depend on what stage you are in life.

It's now known you can also put fear in others. ishould find a way to let him know.

You can find that the mind can travel farther than sight.

Fear to me now, sure I can admit that only a few things actually scares me. Not much to death thou.

Hi I'm beza you human or some kind of living being. yet pretty much You're still human without it. HEllo people..my name is bezalel emanuel george. (Beg)I'm the first Black circus owner in the eastern United states, Also the First multi millionaire in my family.

ImFilthy rich if I do say so. Money bizz usa im also listed as one of the up and coming billionaire club members.

My mom always told me dont count what's in the bag before it was full. I guess I had that boss bag to fill.

through good marketing, will power and selling the heck out of merchandise.A capital for capital empire ive set up.

based in north atlanta, georgia. I also do performances wherever money is handled with very large purses

You also can find me on the company website, my videos on all social media platforms.

I'm a 28 years old boss. a philanthropist.

graduated MIT top of my class. Im Lover of mother nature. I do admire the arts...Not just the dark arts.fine art,natural art(mother nature) designer apparel, lover of cosmic stones (gold).

I'm a jack of all trades if i do say if i do say.

A little tech at times or big tech at times.

My father died in a racing accident (the tricity-dragsters final showdown).

He died on the Last lap. As he turned on the scrapper curves. The turns where to sharpe. At the end of the road is a hook turn you can barely see at 500mph in a speedster m 18. He died instantly. His body was never found due to the fuel cells catching fire causing a massive explosion.

I kind of grew up missing something without my dad.

not that my mom didn't do the best she could. You know the advice a dad would give you. like... when i was going to form a rap group the cosmic zoners he would have told me bad idea Not to say my mom didn't do an excellent job.

i didn't play the victim not having a father and all.

I turned out great a Strong craftmanshipper I've become.

Jack of all trades and a little jack of all magic too.

Spending my days and nights here or there. Usually nights of partying or a gas station explosion or two. I've flound a way to cope with fear;admittingly though i still haven't came to grip with fear. Let a dog catch you off guard with a loud woof! You're gonna jump hopefully not through the roof.

Believe it or not you're actually scared in that brief moment. Fear and a lil gothica is how I get my bags of cash. Fear is everywhere I just make cash of it. scaring folk is my grass roots i'd say... my bread and butter Let's say a fearful fellow in a bar fight...let's say Guy spills a drink on him and tells him he's the blame. He's heart surly is pounding through his chest almost Scared to death. overcoming with a little bit of righteousness he stands his ground.

If he gets beat up who cares.

man or woman you have a moment to be courageous or fearful.

sometimes with help from outside agitators like those from the spirit world puting fear in people. Ninth dimisional spazoid..these entities of the underworld. Evil...i mean pure scume. play man against man, man against nature, evenman against god.

Imagine space..what a void. A unfilled dark void adrifts in a time vortex to algorithms of quantum space. space uncharted...we do have the colony on mars...still do that count.

one minute you could be on a eli musks space x trip around the moon. you can take a planned mining trip on mars I hear they have vacation packages for couples and family.

you can travel beyond as a United states space force cadets the Beyond Mars program is enlisting. The first tour is to the farthest reaches of the milky way. Even though they don't have a space station beyond mars yet. The intern president is hopeful to make it to pluto next term. His democratic rival wants to stop all drilling on the moon as it is hollow and could cause a cosmic ripple in time like we never seen. I'm sure after that we as mankind won't be here to see anything else after that ever.the fear. Sometimes can seem to be everwhere. Even in america we've had a scare mass panic. The toilet tissue is the first to go. I never really understood that. Times like that I call a tissue scare. I do a little skit on that era on my Wednesdays show. We still hold loving memories for all american heroes. There was a pandemic right before I was born. really made the country come together to fight an invisible enemy.which made way for other programs.

Children of AR(after reconstruction) 2030s

the government started mass genos programs

Human antibody experiments.to find the antibody signs that can cure any disease known to man.cosmic pro life vitamin company that exposed a lot of government healthcare low income families to government experimental drugs as part of no citizen without healthcare laws. Healthcare was free and against the law. There were incentives that you had to undergo.

the option to take risky drug trials for a drug manufacturer's for big pharma. It was called the right way programs for underprivlaged minorities. The new world order was an act to make everyone one world citizens. As a citizens of the United States now we were world citizens. With the countries without borders act of 2025. Some women have been exposed to high levels of cosmic energ.

due to the fact a pharmaceutical company started harvesting its plants for its prenatal vitamins on a cosmic rock mound. The large object hit earth million of years ago. Due to climate change and storms over the centuries it was covered by dirt and mud. The earth mound consumed the cosmic energy and minerals and where from there the seeds were layed.the cosmic energy went into the plants.

I know big tech or military tech companies wish they got their hand on those plants.

If they only knew what power they had in hand .

At the time I'm sure the military would have a new super soldier killing machine they can use as a weapon.

At first children of AR seemed normal. Wellmost of us were normal. But some of us have the ability to do amazing things. Like me I can shoot cosmic energy out my hands and I blow things up from time to time. I'm also very smart. I can make things disappear by just switching the object from dimension to dimension. Children of ar(the after reconstruction)

An era that dawned in children with special abilities. Like some could organize a string of robberies unheard of at the time. Like two banks with the missing roof the surveillance shows two children of ar. Yes some are criminals bad guys.

Fear is one of the factors that can give strength tothe thing you fear. being scared.FEAR IS ThE EXPECTATION OF SOMETHING

THAT COULD HAPPEN.FEAR IS THE POSSIABLITY OF SOMETHING THAT COULD CAUSE HARM,PAIN,SADDNESS,or ANY harm to the body(temple). TO THREATEN THE EXSISTANCE OF A BEINGS LIFE,liberty,or ones right to exists. BEing SCARED OR FRIEIGHTEN by the sight of something such as blood and guts is very common. think a bit about it how the sight of blood and guts or any internal organ of a living creature makes some people want to vomit. nausea feeling of being very uncomfortable. IN A WORLD THAT IS AWAKENED and full of demons.

I stand in my corner of atlanta georgia.

I fight evil.. Sometimes some demonic mother loving zombie is walking around in some poor soul's body. And this is living posed by evil. althogh the higher precentage of these are simmingly always the rich ones.

Think about it...you die.they have your funeral the whole works.

Your body is buried in a nice casket in your In family burial plot. Supposidly there not to ever move again. THEn the DEAD ONES HAVE BEEN MORNED BY THEIR FAMILYS AND

BURIED DEEP IN THE GROUND. Then one day at the mall a mom sees her dead son walking with intent. She can't believe it. Most of the time they surge it off as a look alike. Sometimes they go looking..and that's when i come in. Smelling really bad a corpse needs hydro or a fresh blood supply to calm the rotting corpse smell.demons have the DEAD BODY dripping in expensive fragrance and fine lining. Most are rich imposters. They feed on human flesh. I mean the bloodier ther better. also human chi.

Chi is the energy of the soul.some say its the energy around atoms. First came to knowledge in americas in the 2020s. the soul leaves the body some say that energy returns to sender which is god. as were tought in church. What I learned in the streets was EVIL sometimes needs TO FEED ON LIVING FLESH TO MAINTAIN THe NESSARY ENERGY. these are the zombie hord. Demons canmake a zombie hords out of everybodyand anything.

THE SOUL HAS AN ENERGY OF ITs OWN. LIKE A BATTERY sometimes it can be replaced. Yep ima stay my ass right here in atlanta georgia. With a dark magic and cosmic energy that surrounds us all. I'm your horror show/blogger with the most hosts with the mostest. Right here at your locally black owed circus outside ATL georgia.things do get a lil hot and humid in atlanta GA,yet still my SMALL CORNER OF THE WORLd is the only place for me.i dont think i can sell my fireworks anywhere else since i got banned by several states for the amont of power my fireworks display. A little cosmic help and you get a bigger bang.As YOUNG MAN trained in martial arts. my mom comes from the country and moves to a big city to raise me and my sister. Working at ray's chicken as a waitress and at the local circus owned by baker brothers bizarre inc. where Mr baker gave me the circus after a fire.one thing about people around my age is where connected. I banned my community with a couple music and private donations. I got this old thing up and running. He took the insurance money and told me if I could fix it up I could have the dump. Man i worked my tail off to get this circus up and running. I dont

boost my position as owner. After all it was my organizing that got the funds together to remodel the place. Proud to say I even got my own show.

the
Voodoo King clown of horror
an they mystic arts show
4515 dairy milk lane, georgia 07019
Show hrs mon-fri and on
halloween and special events
rules to be admitted
The show is to the left the ride is to the right
enterat your own risk
Food is provided | alcohol is served 21+
Dear patron if you are at risk of a heart
attack not admittance to the show
Not responsible for any personal
item that get damaged
where not liable for you...
please notice all exit signs
In case of fire.

CHAPTER 1

King Clown

The scary part about what I do, isnt the demon slayer or the countless times ive almost died.hell fighting evil beings dont put as much fear in me. No no it's the constent code violation by Atlanta building and development. Im black 28 yr old southern millionaire. They thought I was doing something illegal at one of the random inspections by none other than Delorus bitterbottom county zoning manager. I mean you won't believe what it took to get chicken wings up here. It's still hard at times as a business owner. I'm the first black circus owner in east atlanta georgia. No one thought I'd pull it off. The First Emmy award winning choreographer in my family. My horror show is lit.very popular. I got trending on social media and youtube. My youtube fans are in the millions. Yep..the world they love me. Well the horror show biz. El horror is my number one selling t-shirt. I scare people out of their bottoms

3

sometimes. I create gadgets and other things which I make a ton of money off of.

I live to vanquish evil in all its forms. My setup is Well organized and elaborate while trying to cover it all up to fight evil. My t-shirt sale game is through the roof. You can get your voodoo king made in the USA black and white striped shirts or bags on sale in the gift shop or order online. You gotta have money if you wanna have the impact on some of the evil coming your way sometimes. My mom taught me dark magic. She was a creole country girl. Fishing and horseback riding what she loved. She could sow with the best seamstresses.Loving her church she made me and my sister go to church every sunday. Seeing a good heart is a good way to fight evil she always said. Like abra kadabrah a energy spell.This spell my mom taught me one summer morning. Understanding how to use abra kadabra. You must first understand yourself when she taught me how to control my power. This particular summer I mastered the technique. High School taught me the makeup and blood and guts. First time I saw the dead rising to walk on earth was high school. Children are always the toughest in certain situations. We all will die one day. In death most people say rest in peace. What If,dew33 Emmanuel George gonna be right here to defend my neck of the woods. I feel loved in sunny yet hot georgia wouldnt imagine owning my black owned circus anywhere else. The government would call in the national guard if they knew what I had under the elephants of Carthage Arts exhibate and show. I do think the government would trip if a 10 foot firey demon that onlyelephant courage and sex appeal only extinguishes. I make a great deal of the elephant tshits as well.

A possessed body not born again with a living soul; but an evil demon possessed roiting corpse decaying. I mean they have to be Rich. I'm only saying if demons were poor. The world would be like one of those zombie shows in the 20s. One actually happened and was a coverup by the government and made to look like a show but they were in venezuela. dark spirit controlled by evil. Angry and hateful full of malice with a hunger to eat the living for fresh blood and living flesh. To sustain the demon's control over the body it must give the body something.

The fact that these bodies need to sustain mobility and stability in this dimension has to perform a basic instinct of all living things: the energy of the body with the brain's electrical activities that is embedded in our DNA by invisible strings. We must eat to live. That's why I'm up nights taking care of the family business. Feeding on living everynight.

Looking down at the dirt. I'm dusty and dirty with my face just bouncing off the ground. Thinking everything out that led up to this slowmotion life moment.Thinking of my college friend that i could see from afar.Hes looking at me now the scream sends chills up my spin. Sitting here on the ground with my face in the dirt. Looking around thanks to the huge campfire lighting up the night in the woods. Lighting the way around us as we battle these so-called zombie hord. I look at John, He is being attacked by three zombies. Suddenly one breaks past his guard and before I could get to him he stabs it. Yes..! In the head I am relieved. I wanted to applaud John after killing that one with a knife to the head.before i could tow more where heading my way. Two more were on him also. Before I could have helped him I had two demons that knocked me down. Overwhelmed at the time. I blasted them suckers up with cosmic blasts. They were incinerated in seconds. I hear chumping and blood sucking. As I turn back toward the direction of Jon. I hear their jaws chopping as I roll over to face them. I aim my double barrel shotgun. I discharged Two loud bangs. The bang rang out loud as I took my time shooting them both in the head. A gush of blood and a mesh fly off the tops of their neck like a dash of water. We've been here far to long after midnight. As i should have known better, to be out here after the celestial moon is in its cycle in this cursed land. This cycle of evil ends as it begins when it's finished or defeated. With this evil hunger has an emptiness and no bottom to set a fill. This evil lingers only here where it can hide in the darkness of the thick forestry and swampy knolls. This place where the nights are flesh biting cold only spirits know it well. The human body can not survive here without a fire or some kind of heat or comfort for too long the brain starts playing tricks on you. Hypothermia sets in then you're done. As I rise I'm too late John's struggle is at an end.john is overrun. Zombies begin diving on Him and begin eating on my bud. They were sucking on my friends bones...help me lord Jesus give me strength.I ran over to where he was.

John was barely living as the zombies ate at his arms and neck. One zombie was eating his intestine and I shot that one. I shot John there.

The body was eaten up with barely anything left of him so he can have peace. I burned the body with an inferno cleanse spell abracadabra I spoke into the air wishing i didnt have to do this. Cause once bitten the body begins to shut down after being attacked by a hord or demon. Dark enzymes attack living cells till the life it inhabits becomes pure evil. The living dead they dont really die. It's a period of sickness. Before death driven by pure madness. Leaving room for another demon to enter the body. It was supposed to be a final stand. I set up this area

Where this circle type battle encampment I set up like a nice barn fire type camp area early that day on my family property in the woods.

I turn to see who else could use a hand everyone is holding their own. I enjoy killing as many zombies as I can. I reload my shotgun after emptying it… on John.

CHAPTER 2

King clown On
my way back

I make money off of scaring people and a lot of it is off marketing and merchandise.King Clown voodoo crowns sell like hot cakes. Just a normal show host who happens to be a voodoo clown possesing cosmic energy with mastering the Comsic energy rays which owns and operates a local circus.Using these powers to create illusions that will scare the pants off of any suburbanite. I mostly keep to myself, always have and always will.

I dont have a sidekick or spiritual mentor at the moment. I am seeing a shrink but that's another story. You know me as the voodoo king clown of horror at your very own first ever black own circus in east atlanta georgia. Most of the time I'm in my trailer waiting on my time to scare some unknowing victim at the scary show. I use paint or either masks as my props,and sometimes fireworks and different magical tricks. Ive learned from my mother as I was growing up. My mother was a good witch. If she was born in an earlier time Some 14th century aristocrat wouldve said.. Burned at the stake. Before I was born she was really into the whole dark magic. Scary a woman with power to shape the cosmos. I mean at the snap of a finger she could clean a room. Yet she always made me clean my room manually. She was a pioneer in fighting evil using magical weapons and spells.

The circus is open from 9am to 11pm. Six days a week with Monday's being closed for repairs of other maintenance.Yep im the first black business owner of a circus in north atlanta georgia.The fun part in the city is After midnight. I'm like a caped crusader protecting the city from evil without a cap. I do have a mask though. I dont us any masks from the show. Someone might recongize me. Yep you guessed it. I fight dark forces secretly throughout the world.

No one has ever personally thanked me for saving them.

Doesnt matter, I still push forward with good work. IT'll all workout for the greater good.

I have a lot of masks I use as props at my show. Mask sales were a poor investment at first when I got into marketing them to consumers. My favorite is the one I keep out of sight, the one I use most to fight demons. It's this ebony wood. Trimed in gold and pearl trimmed along the side. This one that my mom gave me apparently accompanied my ancestor to the new world. This ancient mask has cosmic energy like the sun and moon. It gives off cosmic waves vibrations to help me fight demons. With this mask I can see and fight demons in this dimension.Im able tosend them back to hell with a surge of cosmic electrical energy. Even though the occasional high powered gun action,or some knife action. I'll do just fine to kill vessels of evil from this dimension. Sometimes there's no one thing that can win a battle. Different weapons are needed. With a member of the zombie hord I pretty much use anything I can get my hands. The ebony wood mask I can focus my mind on any demon. The mask creates a Circle prism that surrounds the demon and voila back to hell the go. I also use dark magic spells like abracdbra..or Deny spell which denies a demon access to this world. When using the deny spell. You speak the words voomoos then instantly the spell creates a force that snatches the demon out of a corpse's body. Suddenly the corpse goes limp and drops. No more demons, it's that simply. the demon disappears never to be seen again. Although some of the strong ones come back.

Upper level Demons are fallen angels who were cast down from heaven by God with satan. Then there's the earth born hell bent demon born from evil angels and daughters of man.They are very ugly.The zombie hord uses portals to come to this dimension. Portals are always made by demons or someone using dark magic like a wizard or magician. The hord usually roams by the thousands in hell. Only about a couple hundred can enter one portal at a time without it collapsing. Once the horde come through a portal there dumb as a bag of rocks. They dont think they just crave blood and living flesh. Demons can't be killed like you or me because they're already dead. God destroyed all of them on the earthly plane around the time of the great flood about 65,000 bc i believe. The first covenant with man and god to vanquise any evil in the underworld was in egypt 36,000bc. Then there's the hordes of hell they can be killed or is it evaporated as to say because they're not really alive. Sometimes the hord can posses a dead or living body if placed in one by a higher demon. they infest a dead body then right away the feeding begins and the eternal hungry for living flesh to devoir.

CHAPTER 3

Three days earlier

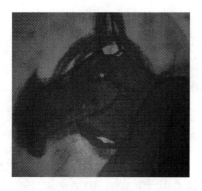

My work trailer isn't what it seems either. Using cosmic energy I can make it disappear or even float in the air. I can move it like a spaceship through the sky. Ive even added different dimensional spaces. My 30ft trailer on the circus grounds just may look like an ordinary trailer with a hitch to the plan eye. With cosmic energy filtered out with spells. My trailer comes equipped with a lab, dining room, an office, training room. I even have a master bedroom in it. My bedroom has a king size bed full bathroom and plenty of closet space for him and hers. I do have a lady. Women need plenty of closet space. My bedroom had more of a king's chamber in medieval time but with a few future pieces. Such as my five 60 inch flat screens. In the training room it's full of ancient and mystical weapons. In the training room I have the fire of hendin which must be kept in a 30 ft air filtering chamber but that is another story. That whole journey was a burst of magical delight. I really upgraded my magical capabilities; the learning curb was full of knowledge in magical spells at that time. The bursts of light momaduch bulls that hit the air when they loved. The guide through a dead mountain guild was a bearded but job who rides the inner mountain mud slops with a flying boat. One of my proud journeys was on hell of a train ride to get to the flames of inner earth. All to get the Kangarian jewel which was at the top of the mountain in a castle. In that dimension the gravity was kind of off how the train was basically flying around curves going up the first mountain. I keep the way to that dimension hidden in a book in my studying chamber. Magic is really a great thing when it comes to consolidation. It really cracks me up to see all the magical capabilities out in the world.

To me it was more than a job but a duty to save the world from real evil.

I really loved my transition from a man to king clown.

I was in my office when my phone rang caller ID read it was my sister. I got a little worried about my sister Morticia calling. I knew something was wrong because my sister never called unless something serious was happening.

As i answersd the phone... Hi Mor

As I swallowed my spit.

Her voice was a little cracking. I could tell she was upset.

Sure was bad news why she called. She told me my mom had died in her sleep last night.

Then she burst into tears…I replied aww calm down sis it's all for the best Mor mom had cancer.

She's in a better place.

This is tough for me though to lose my mom and my bestfriend too.

I told her Lets be strong for mom right now.

As I take a deep breath, I ask her what do you need me to do?

Her reply was "I need you to come down for the funeral."

I've already taken care of all the arrangements for her funeral. Will and trust is the same as she wanted it.

Then she says ' And please show some respect, I really don't want you to screw this up, we only get one time to do this right.

So I have no time for your drama this round beza she states.

My reply was simply "ok" I cleared my throat to say more" Mor I am gonna do everything to give my final respect for my mom she ment the most to me.

Mom was the only person who could make me happy when I was sad.

She also helped me to see what I was to do wow really gonna miss my best friend.

My mom was my comfort she gave me my strength.With her help I elevated into the voodoo king I am today.

Yet still I know there's the potential of the dead rising up to walk the earth with a thirst for blood and guts and all but who really wanna go through dieing. I guess being happy to be with god is better than living. Who knows when but one day we will all die.

An in death who wants their body to be a vessel for evil? Seriously thinking...Not me.

I doubt anyone will. No matter what your beliefs are, whether Christian,Muslium, or buddist whatever. When your soul leaves the body no one wants their bodys not resting in peace walking around with an evil entity .How about the reincarnation factor in beliefs? Who upon being reincarnated enter a new body, and be eaten by your former body over and over again. just imagine a lifeless restless body consumed by evil cursed to roam the earth forever and ever.........
......i'm rudely interrupted by mortecia...WHAT THE HELL!! Are you talking about beza. Just stop with your blaa blaa like you're some smart guy. You're a loser who lucked up and got rich. You have 3 days till momma funeral. Get your act together or dont bother showing up. I look at the phone..wow. Really big sis ok ..Then she inhales then exhales. Saying this as calmly as I possibly can right now. Just listen, I'm going to need you to be on the way...I mean I need you to get here. As soon as possible Ok? I reply that it's all a hurry up on my behalf big sis. Then she hangs up.

Shaking my head I know when my sister's voice begins to crack she is in over her head.

Thinking back at that conversation that night I wondered the rest of the night in the dream world. While wondering in a void pacing cause I still had ground to walk on in this mindle dark void. Mor knew mom was sick and in pain for years. I dont feel as sad she's better off without all that pain. Mom cried everyday about the pain. what she couldn't handle. Mom has been sick for years with lung cancer. I always find a bit of trouble when I go to the country. In them woods of pine and oak rock and stone. Some of the coldest winters with no snow to fall. But there's an evil that lingers there only and only there. Cold dark country woods if the cridders dont get you or the dead cold. In those woods where it can hide in the dark shrubs they can feed on all that tally along its area. where the nights are flesh biting cold. Naw must be something. Just Keep me up all night tossing and turning.

The alarm

6a.m

Up ready to go pay my last respect. Throughout the night I planned out the week trips itinerary. I wanted to visit my family's old house. They had this house about 2miles down a dirt driveway. They even had some old knives that looked really cool the last time I saw them. Even tunnels under the house. where I remembered some of my good childhood memories. I was really fond of the place. The land and cabin was supposed to pass down to my father, but no one wanted it.

CHAPTER 4

Queen Mother be afraid of the voodoo witch

My mom's name was Rachel. She even had a show way back in the day **Voodoo Queen Mother Rachel.** Using that good ole dark magic was the highlight of her show.

I could still remember seeing the sign before the entrance of her show.

I remember the day my mom got this job at the circus. Where she made a living scaring the pants off of people. She gave me the name king clown aka El horror.

Mom had me riding horses with the Grimripper at age 9.

I remember she used to say ''everyone likes the illusion of fear''. As long as it is in a controlled environment''.

People would come for miles and miles around the country to get their scary on.

She tells the crowd "Some people are brave and others go cave diving." Too dark for me to be exploring a cave deep in the darkest parts of the earth. Being scared of the dark for almost all my childhood.It wasnt the darknes that I feared No it was what was in the dark that worried me. My mom Rachel who was a good gatherer of cosmic energy and a good witch made me proud of who she was. She's the one who held a lot of these hell raising demons at bay.ooch i hit my toe while tryna gather my things for the trip. Just to think and stupid cancer takes such a hero from this world. Beza grasps his palm and a Burst of Cosmic rays surround both of his hands glowing with such a power he calms down and doesnt release a cosmic blast.

All morning the next day,Beza could only think back on my mom's life.He thought of the first mask she made for him.Then Beza smiles and rushes to put on his shoes.

Beza says loudly "I need the mask" he ment the mask(Rasun). Which was an ancient egyptian mask. To retrieve the mask Beza says simply "give me my face".Then the el horra mask(mask of rasun) is in his hand. One of the greatest gifts his Mom gave him.

That mask was strong in a cosmic energy disposition efficient full of dark magic.

Suddenly Beza stared off into a daze thinking of mojo.

Mojo was beza childhood demon. Mojo was a demon from ancient celtic tribes. He

hated humans that used dark magic.

Witches were burned at the stake when Mojo did his worst.

My mom protected me from mojo by casting protective spells around the house so mojo could't penetrate the house. Every since mojo discoverd the george family was strong in cosmic energy he has been pursuing them.

Mojo discovered the family while the george family was out camping with his family. Beza remembered what mojo had done to him. Mojo had sniffed beza out,demons like mojo can smell cosmic energy. Mojo lured beza to the middle of the wood with illusions mojo did things to his mind. Mojo touched Beza and saw his cosmic energy. As he was about to eat beza. Mojo disappears as he hears Rachel conjuring spells behind his back to save her child. Mojo was 7 foot and weighed about a ton. Green hair with razor sharp teeth. Mojo skin was a frog green.

Mojo walked like a man, but hated wearing corpses after his physical body was destroyed he would have to possess a human's body. Gaining strength he soon regains his body back after consuming mountain goats and living in caves in mountains. He didnt bother to blend in or cover up. He was the slimest of slim. Big pointy ears and nose. After mojo disappeared beza saw him in glimpses Mojo wanted to eat beza.

Mojo tried attacking beza through the kitchen sink then rachel put a banishment spell on mojo and beza hasnt seen him since.Beza thought to hisself. I remember a very dark spirit hunted me one summer every night. I remember tossing and turning having nightmares. My mom would come into my room in the middle of the night to stop me from yelling about the fearful dreams I had of mojo eating me. and said; I'm gonna show you how to protect yourself. I had told her about mojo and how he said he was always gonna find me and kill me for what my family has done to him my mom would say " no demon got more power then your ole gal right here right now, dont be scared babe"she took me bythe hand into her study.

In the study she went to the book shelf and picked up this decorated box.

It was the el horra mask.

She said here learn to use it and never have to worry about no old bully no more. After that my mind was getting strong. I read more and started tryna understand the el horra mask. How some demons like mojo take over other dead bodies when they are not strong enough to have power in the earthly realm. My first lesson was to ward off evil. Mojo caught me in the dream world. As instructed I spoke the deny spell and like that Mojo never came back.

So I planned to go alone to Baymont, but when I text my friends on group chat after Mor called. Everyone wanted to come be there for me and my family in the morning. Everyone began to show up just as I finished packing.

The doorbell rang. When I got to the door to see it was. I smiled.

It was Smiley the mobile mechanic. He had been checking out my car before the trip.

I asked him " Any bad news" ?

Smiley said "all is good I went on and gave you an oil change, tire rotation. I also made sure your tire pressure and condition was good. I did my 100 point inspections. Your vehicle is at 85% needing minor maintenance soon." smiley takes a deep breath " that'll be $98.99.

I told him to run the debit card he did and was on his way.

Bezas doorbell rang again. He opened the door. It was Jon.

John and beza became friend years ago at the the meditarainan restaurant that was downtown atlanta. Beza worked as a server and John was an up and coming chef. John walks in and heads straight for the kitchen where he immediately starts gubbing out on bezas grocery.

Beza looks and laughs then the doorbell rings again. Beza opens the door to see his old friend Figs and his wife emily.

Figs who smoked a lot of cigs when he and Beza were younger that beza just swapped the S with F and there are figs. The F comes from his real name which was franklin.

I Just started calling him figs. Figs dont smoke cigarettes though i think he seems a bit bubble headed sometimes.figs new everything about beza.

Beza tells them to come in and take a seat they were waiting on others to show up. Fig says ok and closes the door.

Jon walks from the kitchen and says " Hi Beza where's the syrup dude" Beza replies to " top cabinet jon". Jon rushes back to what he was just doin. Figs and his wife and son now work at the circus as tight rope walkers and they do the trapidzo when the bounce of a trampoline then through a hole. Beza even lets them sell their own merchandise at the circus. Part of the contract figs and jon had come up with before figs joined beza at the circus.

I met my girl Taylor at a fig show. She was friends with figs wife Emily who was attending the show for support. Taylor shows up with her brother Chase and friend Jen. we all begin to group up. John comes with this big sandwich. Looking at me as he walked in, John said 'really man the mask' why do you have that man? It looks really cool. Can I try it on? NO was my immediate response. Then figs say you're not at work. Someone sees you with that on you might get arrested or killed or maybe arrested and killed at the same time. We all laugh. My friends know me and they all know who I am. Rachel never told me to hide my abilities from my friends. Kinda cool to be able to impress your friend with some super ability. As we began to get ready for the long drive to sagemont georgia. I tell everyone aloud ' there is evil in the country you don't know about. Please stay close to me if things get a little crazy. John yells out why some of your inbred cousins gotmasked an mistake us as road kill. My girl tells him to shut up and the chase pushes him. I'm beginning to finish packing thinking to myself we're gonna need this mask and more if I'm taking all of them. O yeah and john was my girl taylor's brother as she yells out 'shut up john mom shouldnt have spoiled you and maybe you could be a man not a kid at thirty'. John shrugs his shoulders and says okok ima stop just dont push me anymore sis. Sorry We all get in the cars Taylor,Emily and figs ride together and John and I ride together everyone else are in separate cars. Me and Taylor rode together after we fuel up. I told them before we left "We Are staying at my grandparents house tonight." Everyone was excited to know it was on a lake property. I tell them all this before we leave seems like it was going to be a good trip if the circumstances wasnt so gloomy.

CHAPTER 5

(Receipt to kill a demon possessed corpse: 4 bullfrogs, 3 Green pepper dust from mount nero, an 15 dead flys, 3 blue frogs only there blood, 5 sweet patatos, and dirt)

An hour into the drive to baymont. Morticia calls me on my cell phone. I answer the phone" Hello"

. All I hear is this is mothesa saying" i'm:"sorry about yesterday.""I was very sad. about right now."

"When are you gonna be here? "Almost there was my reply to her. We're staying at our grandparents . old cabin a few minutes from the lake. Is the key still under the white rock.

She answered yes, and she asked who we are? I replied to Taylor and a few of our friends.Figs coming remember figs from the circus he's coming out as well. Mor laugh yeah i remember fig how is he cant wait to see him again. I will be down later. I have a few more things to arrange for the funeral. Mom left you the house and if you want the grands property. Someday just maybe you and Taylor can move here..Possibly raise a family here. Hopefully you can…..someday put the mask and magic away. Mom would have really wanted you

41

to do that. I Told her right out, thanksbut no thanks. I'm gonna love doing shows as I get old. Yet some days it's great. I do have a host of other things I need taking care of. But Never know anything's possible Morticia answers were dark and shallow." see you later then brother be safe. I have things to prepare … routines to run…talk to you later. It takes us 2hr to get their several gas and rest stops later we arrive in famous sagemont georgia. best of places to visit in the united states, id say its woody pine heaven be the. My parents inherited the horse and cabin on the lake from my grandparents. It has a stable, also cabin and boating dock on the corner of lake congaree….. Yeah big boating on the congaree river in the summer fresh game in the summer. I remember fishing in the summer; these trips when mom was too busy with her show. Dad always was preparing for each show. My dad Jack Clarkson was an electrician for the entire circus grounds which had to provide maintenance service for the entire 5 acre circus compound…..things were kind of calm on the lake which was residential mostly.

Finally we arrived. It looked the same..nice just as i remember it. We drive up to the cabin and a lot of feelings come back as if something was out of place. I begin to tell everyone don't touch anything inside the cabin's basement, that is things that were shut and locked sealed shut, an dont touch my mom's things. Looking at fig.. Hi, Fig morthesa stopping by later she really wants to see you. Fig reply ole mort cool can't wait to see sis again we really had a fun childhood growing up our families did everything together.fig reply was" I remember staying the night with you an mort turning me into a chicken."" Your mom had to change me back but the only thing to change me back was to make me a chicken egg first". We both burst out laughing. Everyone gets out of the cars at once as we parked. John say" it looks good to be close to the lake. `houses were creepy. Taylor pushes John again. I laugh no doubt bro it's just a hold creepy looking cabin. It's been in the family for years. I haven't been down lately to fix it up. I tell john ' one last thing once i fix it up i'll sell it to you for cheap. John's reply was simple but not sweet' yeah if you pay me to tear this one down and build another one. Fig steps in and says' john really it's very nice wish my family was able to pass me this down. I look around for the house guard, the infamous white rock with the key under it. I find the rock in its usual place, get the key and we all enter the house. I feel this weird feeling like one of those western where they're about to be a dual. And the dead gust of wind comes out of nowhere and stops everyone in their tracks. And we all got really tight next to each other until the swift breeze stopped. I tell everyone to have their pick of which room they were going to be sleeping in tonight and meet back in the kitchen after we all get settled. Everyone says ok and we go our separate ways into the house. Fig and Emily go into a room and begin to kiss. Fig says " i wanted to kiss you all day".emilys reply " I know we only hooked up last week. I really care for you a lot Emily's reply yes as she kisses fig on the cheeks. I really love you fig. I wanna marry you and have your kids and live in your circus trailer with you. they both lay down in the bed. Taylor and Chase are in the kitchen putting up the supplies. Chase said to taylor; this is a really nice sad circumstance but a little paint and fix up a few boards this would be really nice. Jen finds a room after riding all the way here arguing with john. She begins to unack in one of the rooms upstairs.

I was upstairs unpacking me and taylor things. Jen stops in the room with John and says' your sister boyfriend really scares me sometimes with the things he can do. And all the trouble and danger he has put us through over the years. John laughs a bit and grabs Jen and says' he has been through a lot. I give the guy a hard time but he's really a good guy and tries to help. And he laughs even though he is a moron. I don't think he means any harm to you or anyone. Jen replied' remember how he insinuated that demon in the sewers who kidnapped that kid. John's reply was; and if it wasn't for those who know what would have happened. Let me rephrase that last statement' he's no harm to the living unless provoked. I think he'll protect my sister. Let's go downstairs and meet up with the guys with nothing to worry about. He directs her out his room and down the stairs in the kitchen where Taylor and Chase are just finishing unpacking supplies an began drinking. Beza comes down then comes fig and emily. Emily and fid huggin an snuggle so bad that taylor noticed in shock cause neither of them told anyone they were hooking up.

Beza pulls up a chair and everyone begins to sit. Kc had his head down and Taylor began to comfort him. Kc says' i really wish i was here for my mom more in the end. Taylor comforts him by saying' you did a great job as a son and she will always love you……………...everyone becomes still and quiet when that breeze comes. Came swiftly back all of a sudden with a faint whisper it seemed only i could hear………………..' i killed your mother now im gonna kill you. '... I jumped from the table. And I screamed out what if mojo killed her!.......No one said a word.

After dinner we all decided to have a couple drinks. We played card games and laughed about old times.

Outside smoking meant taylor was in the outdoor loveseat hanging rocker. We shared the rest of the bottle of wine. Taylor turned to me and said what did you mean; earlier when you freaked out. I'm sure your mom knew how much you loved her.

Mojo is just a figment of your imagination. There hasn't been a report of any demon that strongly believes me. I've checked beza.

I put it simply and calmly: I think mojo killed here. As a child I tried to forget about that summer when he tormented me in my dreams and caused havoc in my life. Let me show you something taylor; pulling a book off the table on demon worship. After turning to the folded pages; i set it as a bookmark. There is a picture of mojo; it tells how he is a top level demon of the dead and the living. Demonic spirits like mojo want the world to burn. Underneath these hounds of hell. Taylor continued reading.

CHAPTER 6

Mojones just been waiting for the right time, he's immortal. Time for battle team; team work makes a dream work.

12:01 everyone was relaxing and enjoying the trip. Even though the circumstances are sad they enjoy themselves. Jen and John are on the couch kissing in the living room cuddling under the fireplace that is in front of them. While looking into eachother eyes they hear a noise that startles them.

Johns says "What the heck am I paranoid about?"" Did you hear that?"

Jen jumps up from slouching yea. what was that?

Looking in the direction John points and says "It came from outside."

John quickly says ' somebody might be tryna break in the car. Some country basic fools tryna steal the radio or something. Let's check it out hun.

Jon rushes outside where Taylor and Beza are looking toward the car because they heard the noise too. John and Beza go to where the cars were parked with the flashlight in hand. Beza sees on both cars tires were flat. The group stood in shock because it looked like something had clawed the side of each vehicle. Jon yells got dahm man i just got those tired two weeks ago they were 1200 for the set....its mojo i said in uncertainty... John came rushing at me and we began to tussle as the rest of the group broke us up. Not right now dude jon is screaming. Not right now dude you brought us out here; and now we're stuck. Jon continues to yell in frustration. Taylor says break it up guys..

Jen was looking close at the tires and said' there's no nails it's like somebody squeezed the air out the tires. Fig bends down in agreement and says ' whatever did this was deliberately is all i know. And very strong. Beza and Jon are finally broken up and Jon says i know a tire place we can go to get them fixed. They have towing and are not that far. Jon says ok. The Story man just got pissed off. Fig tells Emily ' lets go back inside out here is giving me the creeps. They both go inside.

Later that night after the rest of the group came in from doing more investigation and finding nothing. Everyone is resting for the next day.

In the room fig and Emily are laying in bed asleep; Mojo is standing over them. As they jump up to hear the others down stairs mojo is gone. They decide to accompany everyone outside.

It is revealed in minutes that by Possessing dead bodys to control Mojo has erected a zombie horde and then they begin attacking everyone in the group. One dives down out of the tree and grabs Emily by the throat and bits her face. Fig awaken by these actions attempts to get the zombie off of Emily who is yelling. The group begin a fight for their lives with fighting abilities they never knew they had. As screams fade away everyone rushes in the house and finds Fig beating the zombie with a branch by the door that had bitten emily.

John yells let's get out of here after the group settles up down stairs. Jen says the tires are slashed. Fig and Beza bring Emily down stairs after helping calming her down upstairs. They sit her down in the living room; to put bandages on her wounds. Taylor sits beside Emily and tries to comfort her. A loud bang at the door startles the group when the door comes crashing down more zombies rush into the living room. They begin fighting the zombies; gabbing anything they can find near them. Two zombies carry Emily outside after pushing Taylor down. Beza rushes to a sealed room and grabs a shotgun and more weapons and begins handing them out. They rush outside where the demons are holding Emily down and they begin fighting them off with a stick. Jen fights saying "I never seen anything like this" meanwhile more demon possessed zombies come out the woods in droves. John gripping a knife says "let's call the cops there more equipped to handle things like this". Beza laughs to himself . Chase says " if something happens to me you're going to the electric chair" my dads gonna make sure of that. Cocking back the trigger on a double barrel I aim and shoot as many zombie hordes as I can. Beza fires a couple cosmic blasts. Taylor fires her hand gun. Looking at jon ' kc say ' you wait on the cops i'll kill all these bastards before they get here. An beza and the group starts to open up a can of whoop ass on the demons blowing heads off with weapons they got from beza. The rest of the group joins in and it begins.

CHAPTER 7

Defending against mojo mojo It begins where we ended

After seeing John die the group gather himself and take his body back inside. Standing over John, I'm looking around. Everyone is covered in blood and everyone was hurt. I'm screaming ' jon come on man pull through and Taylor is holding his hand. Fig say' what are we going to do? My girl is hurt. She needs a hospital. He was standing up holding Emily up. ' the tires are flat, the phones aren't working, what the hell are we going to do.

Taking a little time to collect myself. I walk towards chast who was looking outside to see if any more demons were coming. ' hey chase help my put this door back up.' we do just that. ' ought to keep them away for a minute or so i know more are coming we must find mojo and stop him. Kc goes into his mother's spell room an grabs some portion. Why getting the porton the woman begins holding jon body down as it begin to shack as he foams out the mouth. Mojo appears an the woman step back mojo lifts john body up an he begins to shake even more. Kc yells out a spell a jon awakens as he is floating in the air. Mojo attempts to squeeze the life out of jon. As he is looking at kc the zombies come crashing into window, underfloor boards, knocking the door down the group a about to be overwhelm as the fight off hell's army of demons. Emily and fig are protected with cosmic energy blasters by Beza as they are being surrounded by demons.

They begin blasting away at the hounds of hell back to hell. Beza yells at Taylor ' catch this ' after seeing she needed more ammo and Taylor catches the valve of potion and she knew what to do. Taylor splashed the potion on mojo and said a spell. Mojo disappears and releases john beza rushes over and pours another potion in johns mouth he is awakened and says; hey guys, in a delusional way. Taylor say we got you john. Beza looks at him and says' ' sorry man for earlier I thought you were a gonner. John has no clue of what's going onhow beza had killed him and mojo possessed his body for a while. john looks down and sees blood on his shirt and passes out. Beza yells' john john " seeing that he was breathing jen says he fainted yall he'll be ok. Everyone looks at Taylor who was a nurse puts her hand near his nose and chest. Yes as she breathes deeply she says slowly " he's ok" as she noticed he was completely healed "jens right he's just passed out"

Then a loud crackle! Mojo appears again and the group stands up and says go back to hell demon. They all begin to shoot their guns at him, beza firing cosmic energy bursts from his hand. They begin to destroy Mojo who was falling back.

Then Mojo yells out "comtula"! The whole group is shocked with demon magic and knocked down. And where being held down with the demon magic some kind of invisible force. While on the ground kc noticed mojo coming towards him to finish him. While separately shocking the the others with cosmic energy from his hands mojo says your family has stopped me for the last time not i end this tonight. Revenge is mines. Yes i killed your mom; i snuck in a took her breath away she was too weak to stop me in her old age. Mojo began to laugh, causing agony and havoc to everyone in the room. Beza sees a glimmer of hope and lures mojo closer.beza says to mojo" It was easy to keep you at bay all these years you ugly weak demon."" You will always lose, you're on the losing side. That's how it's gonna be forever; someone will always be here to stop you."Mojo has finally made his way to Beza, by floating through the air. Mojo says "your one of them heros huh?" "ive been hearing of these types of human rebellion" everyone is still in agony on the floor unable to stand up. Beza says " give me my face and the el horra mask appears. Beza laughs as mojo grabs him. In his right hand Beza has his mask and puts on. Mojo drops him hard to the floor and Beza says the deny spell mojo tries to flee but the mask holds him in one spot. Beza free from the demon magic pulls out a dante knife. And say "hey! Mojo you know what this is?" Mojo says nothing but he has this very uncomfortable look on his face. Mojo looks with a whole lot of fear and anger but the invisible force of the mask holds him. Beza stabs the knife through the mojo head. Mojo body explodes all the rest of the group gets up after mojo hold on them is over. Everyone shows signs of relief as mojo,the demon horde is gone immediatly.

The sun begins to rise its morning as the group steps outdoor its morticia pulling up looking in shock.

After everyone is taken to hospital ; the one who could make it to the funeral. We put mom to rest with pride that her killer has been destroyed.

We all settled up at morticia house after the funeral to eat and say our goodbyes. We've all had our fill of this town for a while. After we ate and chatted we loaded up into the cars to head back home to north atlanta. As I was pulling off I said to taylor. Morticia seems alright to you? She says" yes she just been through a lot you know how your dad died and she was looking a certain staring off in a daze for days." Yeah I guess you're right i replied to taylor and drove off. Half way down the road, Beza makes a promise to taylor to visit his sister more. "She'll be ok." he keep on telling hisself

Later that night at Morticia's house there is a deep underground basement that leads to a cave. Inside the cave is morticia. In a trance Morticia speaking spells with candles burning along a ceremony circle. Morticia is dressed in a black robe. Chanting to bring back mojo chanting. Mojo's voice is faint and says' i will return to you my child.

The end

Printed in the United States
By Bookmasters